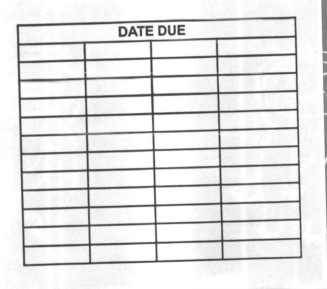

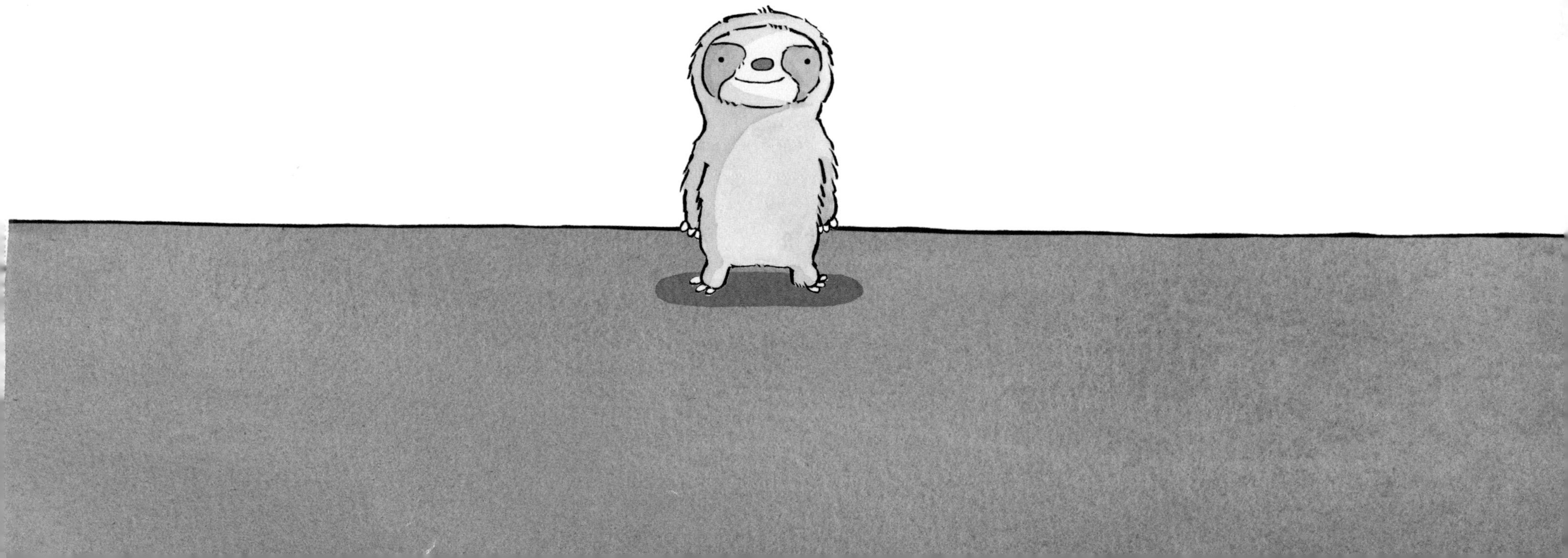

Sloth is about to do

Whee! Falling letters!

For Mom and Dad, Who Always Encouraged My Stories, Silliness, and Tolerated My Gazelling—C. A. F. V.

For Ronan and Luke, two of the best things in the world—R. C.

First Edition

GREENWILLOW BOOKS

in the world.

Mervin the Sloth is about to do

the best thing in the world.

the best thing in the world.

the best thing in the world.

the best thing
in the world.

the best thing in the world.

the best thing in the world.

Hug his